Usborne First Experiences
Going to a Party

Anne Civardi

Illustrated by Stephen Cartwright

Edited by Fiona Watt
Cover design by Neil Francis

There is a little yellow duck hiding on every double page. Can you find it?

This is the Dunn family.

Nellie is five and Ned is three. Ned has a black and white puppy called Harvey.

A party invitation arrives.

Pete, the postman, gives Nellie a big letter. It is an
invitation to Larry White's party on Saturday.

They make fancy dress costumes.

Larry is having a fancy dress party. He wants all his friends to come dressed as monsters.

Granny helps to make two monster costumes. But Grandpa is being a bit of a nuisance.

Mrs. Dunn takes Nellie and Ned to the toyshop to choose a present for Larry. Nellie wants to buy him a robot.

They are ready to go.

On Saturday Ned and Nellie get dressed in their costumes. They are ready to go to the party.

They arrive at the party.

Mrs.
White

Mr.
White

Larry

Nellie gives Larry his present. He is six years old today.
The cat is frightened of Ned.

Lots of other monsters have already arrived. They all try
to guess who is wearing each mask.

Larry opens his presents.

All Larry's friends have brought him a present. He is very pleased with the robot from Nellie and Ned.

Mrs. White writes a list of who gave him each present.
He has lots of thank-you letters to write tomorrow.

There are lots of things to eat.

At last it is time to eat. Mrs. White has made all kinds of delicious things.

Larry has a chocolate birthday cake with a ghost on top.
Do you think he can blow out all his candles in one go?

They play party games.

After tea there are lots of games to play. It is Nellie's turn to pin the tail on the pig.

Ned wins first prize for the best fancy dress costume.
All the other monsters win prizes as well.

It's time to go home.

The party is over. It is time to go. Mr. Dunn comes to collect Nellie and Ned.

This edition published in 2005 by Usborne Publishing Ltd, Usborne House, 83-85 Saffron Hill, London EC1N 8RT, England.
Copyright © 2005, 1992 Usborne Publishing Ltd. www.usborne.com
First published in America in 2005. UE
The name Usborne and the devices ♀ ⊕ are Trade Marks of Usborne Publishing Ltd.